Trouble at Table 5

at Table 5

#2:
Busted by Breakfast

Check out all the
TROUBLE at TABLE 5
books!

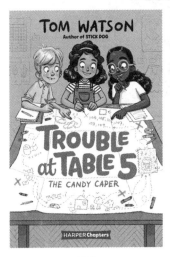

#1

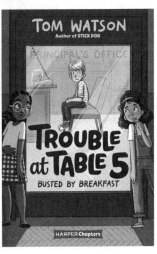

#2

Read more books by **Tom Watson**

#1–12

#1–5

TROUBLE at TABLE 5

#2:
Busted by Breakfast

by **Tom Watson**

illustrated by
Marta Kissi

An Imprint of HarperCollins*Publishers*

Dedicated to Elizabeth
(IASPOY)

Trouble at Table 5 #2: Busted by Breakfast
Text copyright © 2020 by Tom Watson
Illustrations copyright © 2020 by HarperCollins Publishers
Illustrations by Marta Kissi
Library of Congress Control Number: 2019950274
ISBN 978-0-06-295344-5 — ISBN 978-0-06-295343-8 (pbk.)
Typography by Torberg Davern
20 21 22 23 24   PC/LSCC   10 9 8 7 6 5 4 3 2 1

First Edition

Table of Contents

CHAPTER ONE
Soggy-CRUNCH!
Soggy-CRUNCH!

THERE ARE TIMES when Simon just cannot be quiet. He has to talk. And there is no way he can stop until he's done telling us everything.

That's what happened yesterday.

In Mr. Willow's class.

At Table 5.

Simon got to school later than us because Rosie and I rode bikes and he walked.

Simon broke his bike. He rode it on the rock trail at Picasso Park, but it isn't the kind of bike that's made for that. It has thin tires for streets and sidewalks, not thick tires with bumps on them for trails and stuff.

So the bike got all busted up. It has two flat tires and the wheel rims are bent.

"Molly! Rosie!" Simon called to us when he hurried into the room. He was excited about something, I could tell. Rosie could tell too. He kicked his backpack under the table and sat down. "Do you guys know what Cocoa Puffs are?!"

We nodded.

"Well, I didn't know what they were until today," Simon began. "They're little brown, ball-shaped, sugary dynamos of chocolaty goodness. The great thing about Cocoa Puffs is the whole eating *process*.

It's like three scrumptious chocolate discoveries in one."

We just stared at him. He was pretty excited. He couldn't wait to tell us more. And the more he spoke, the faster his words came out.

"The first several mouthfuls of Cocoa Puffs start out super crunchy," he explained. "The first burst of chocolate flavor is like CRUNCH! BAM! WAKE UP! It's chocolate time! That's the first

discovery. But then, about halfway through the bowl, all the Cocoa Puff balls have absorbed some milk and they've started to lose their crunchiness. And, you know, that's kind of a bummer. Because who wants to eat soggy stuff?"

Simon stopped to lick his lips and then continued.

"And here's what you think: Oh no! My delightful chocolate dream has turned into a terrible chocolate nightmare. Instead of crunchy Cocoa Puffs, I've got half a bowl of soggy, mushy Cocoa Puffs."

He was talking even faster now.

"The disappointment starts to wash over you. Maybe it's time to dump them into the sink. But that would be wasteful, so you take a few more bites and—WHAM!—you make the second chocolate discovery!"

When Simon inhaled, Rosie cut in and asked, "What's the second discovery?"

"The chocolate balls *look* and *feel* soggy on the outside—but they're still crunchy and sugary on the *INSIDE*!" Simon exclaimed.

He was louder now. Some of our classmates stared back at our table.

"I mean, WHAT?! Are you kidding me?! Can you even be serious?! My chocolate nightmare is a crunchy chocolate dream again?! That's impossible. But it's not!"

His voice was *really* loud now. "You feel and taste the evidence each time you chew," Simon almost yelled. "*Soggy*-CRUNCH! *Soggy*-CRUNCH! *Soggy-soggy*-CRUNCH-CRUNCH!"

The bell rang.

The school day started.

But, umm, Simon wasn't finished yet.

YOU'VE ALREADY READ MORE THAN 50 SENTENCES. OFF TO A GREAT START!

1

CHAPTER TWO

MR. WILLOW'S FOOTSTEPS

"IT'S SURPRISING! IT'S amazing! You finish the second half of that bowl even faster than the first," Simon said as the rest of the class sat down and got quiet. He didn't even notice.

"And then—OH NO!—the nightmare is back! The chocolate balls are gone. You ate them too fast! There's nothing left. You didn't savor the flavor.

All you have now is the fading memory of chocolaty scrumptiousness. Then you—"

"Simon, the bell—" I tried to interrupt. But he didn't pay any attention. He had to keep going.

"Then you make the third amazing discovery!"

The whole room was quiet.

Except for Simon.

And Mr. Willow's footsteps.

"Simon, here comes—" Rosie said, trying to stop him.

It didn't work.

"You didn't even notice!" Simon continued, even louder. "It's the milk!"

Mr. Willow stood behind Simon.

Simon didn't know he was there.

"It's brown!" Simon yelled.

He sort of stood up halfway and leaned toward Rosie and me with his hands on the table. "Beautiful chocolaty brown! You sip and slurp and swallow every last drop of that liquid chocolate treasure!"

Simon sat down. He exhaled.

He whispered, "And that—that—is the Cocoa Puffs breakfast experience."

Some of the kids in class applauded.

Mr. Willow did not.

He put a hand on Simon's shoulder.

"Come see me at my desk after I take attendance," he said.

That happened Friday.

On Saturday, Rosie and I headed to Simon's house.

TWO CHAPTERS DOWN. YOU MUST BE FOCUSED!

CHAPTER THREE

ROSIE FIGURES IT OUT

WHEN WE GOT to Simon's house, he was sitting in his garage. Simon was criss-cross applesauce on the hood of his mom's blue Toyota Camry.

He did not look happy.

"So?" Rosie asked. "What happened?"

"Principal Shelton called my parents," Simon said. "She said my mouth gets me into too much trouble at school."

"It does," Rosie said and laughed a little.

"I mean, when you get talking like that, there's no stopping you."

"I know, right?" Simon admitted. "I wish I could stop. It's just once my mouth gets going, then my brain starts going too. And it's like they both work together super fast. And I can't stop until I get everything out."

"I get that," I said. And I really did. I know what it's like to be totally concentrated on something.

It was like that time I had to—I just *had* to—know how many Skittles were in that jar on Principal Shelton's desk. "What did your parents say?"

"She only talked to my mom," Simon explained as he slid off the hood of the car. He brushed off his pants. The car was dirty. "Dad's out of town. He had to go to Cincinnati for work."

"What did your mom say?" Rosie asked.

"She wasn't too upset. But she said I have to tell Dad right when he gets home," Simon answered. "Like the moment he gets out of the car."

"When does he get home?" Rosie asked.

"Today."

"Today?" I asked.

"Today," Simon confirmed, shaking his head.

I could tell he thought he would get punished—like super punished. He kicked a deflated soccer ball into the garage. The garage was full of stuff and totally messy.

"I think he's going to be pretty mad," Simon said.

"It will be okay," I said. I wanted to make him feel better.

"I don't think so," Simon said. "Dad had to work on the weekend. He has to drive all the way here from Cincinnati—on a Saturday. He's going to be tired and grumpy when he gets out of the car. And I'll be right there to tell him I got into trouble at school."

It was bad. All three of us knew it.

But then Rosie started to twirl her hair around her left index finger. She was thinking.

Simon noticed too.

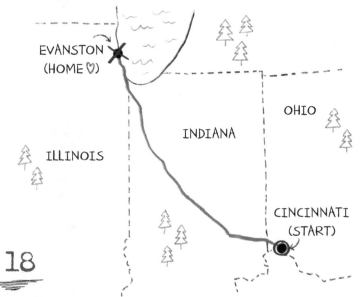

EVANSTON
(HOME ♡)

OHIO

INDIANA

ILLINOIS

CINCINNATI
(START)

"You have to tell your dad as soon as he gets out of the car, right?" Rosie asked Simon. She wasn't looking at him. She was looking in the garage as she twirled her hair.

"Yeah," Simon answered slowly.

"And he's going to be in a bad mood?"

"Probably."

"So," Rosie said, turning away from the garage and toward us. "What if when he gets out of the car, the garage is totally clean? And your mom's car is washed and shiny? Would that change his mood?"

Simon opened his eyes wide. He liked the idea immediately.

"He would be totally surprised!" Simon said and smiled. "And totally happy. He's always talking about what a mess this is, but there's never time to clean it up."

Simon hesitated for a few seconds. He stared into the garage, turning his head from left to right.

"But Mom said he's going to be home around dinnertime. There's no way I can get this done by then."

Rosie looked at me.

I looked at Rosie.

And we looked at Simon.

Then Rosie and I said the same thing at the same time.

"You're not going to do it by yourself!"

CHAPTER FOUR

SIMON'S DAD GETS CLOSER

WE NEEDED TO get to work.

"We should wash the car first," Rosie said quickly. "Can you get your mom to pull it into the driveway? That will also empty the garage and give us more room to work."

"And more room to see what we have to do," I said.

Simon went to get his mom.

Simon's mom came out and said it was

really nice of me and Rosie to help him with the garage. She said to come get anything we wanted in the kitchen. And she said Simon wasn't really in a lot of trouble with her. She used to talk too much in class too.

She also said it was a smart idea to wash the car and clean the garage. She thought Simon's dad would love it.

"But it's no guarantee that Simon won't get punished," she said.

Then she pulled the blue Toyota Camry out of the garage.

"How long will it take Dad to get home?" Simon asked his mom as she got out of the car.

"From Cincinnati? About six hours," she answered and then snapped her fingers.

"I tell you what, I'll track his car on my phone and let you know where he is."

"Is he taking I-74 to I-65?" I asked.

Simon's mom tilted her head to the left and said, "What?"

I could tell she wasn't saying *What?* because she didn't hear me. She was saying *What?* because it was a weird question for me to ask.

"This might sound strange," I said. "But I—"

Rosie interrupted. "Molly has a thing with maps."

"It's just who she is," Simon added. "It's totally cool."

25

"When we take a long trip in the car, I need to know what towns we're going to pass through," I explained. "And in what order. Because if I don't know what's next, I mean, anything could happen."

Simon's mom untilted her head and nodded. I think she was just being polite

and trying to show that she understood. Even though I don't think she did.

"Anyway, we had to go to my aunt's wedding a few years ago in Shelbyville, Indiana," I continued. "So I know all the cities and towns on the main highways in Indiana."

"Isn't that awesome?!" Simon exclaimed.

His mom asked, "If Dad's coming from Cincinnati, what towns will he pass through?"

I looked up at the sky for a few seconds. The answer was stuck in a different part of my brain, so I had to find it. Aunt Kate's wedding was, you know, three years ago.

When I found it, I said, "Batesville, Greensburg, Shelbyville, Indianapolis, Lebanon, Lafayette, Remington, Crown Point, Hammond, Chicago. Then, here, Evanston."

Simon's mom just stared at me. She didn't say anything, but Simon did.

"Like I said," he exclaimed and pointed at me. "Awesome!"

Simon's mom got out her phone, opened an app, and tracked down the car.

EVANSTON
HOME

LAKE
MICHIGAN

CHICAGO

HAMMOND

CROWN POINT

ILLINOIS

REMINGTON

LAFAYETTE

OHIO

LEBANON

INDIANAPOLIS

SHELBYVILLE

GREENSBURG

BATESVILLE

INDIANA

CINCINNATI
START

29

She said, "He's between Batesville and Greensburg."

"We better get started," Simon said. "Like, right now."

CHAPTER FIVE

THAT'S NOT MY GRANDMA

SIMON FOUND A bucket with sponges and soap on one of the garage shelves and we washed the car.

I would like to tell you that something super interesting happened while we washed the car. You know, like it became a big water fight or something. But nothing like that happened. We just, you know, washed the car.

We couldn't reach the roof, but Rosie figured it out. Simon and I made cups out of our hands by interlocking our fingers. And Rosie put her left foot into my hands and her right foot into Simon's hands. Then we gave her a boost. She washed the car roof that way.

"I'm going to get a monster truck when I'm old enough to drive," Simon said as we dried the car with a couple of old towels. "It will be bright orange.

That's my favorite color. I'll drive it all over town."

"You can't drive a monster truck on the streets," Rosie said as she dried off a headlight. "You'll get arrested."

"I'll just drive it up mountains and stuff then," Simon said. "You know, bash into things on purpose. Roll it over. That kind of thing."

"You're crazy," Rosie said and threw her towel at Simon. "That's how you broke your bike!"

33

"That's true," Simon admitted. "But you can't break a monster truck. They're totally unbreakable!"

I threw my towel at him too. With the car washed, he dropped them both in the bucket. We were done with that part of the job.

Wait.

No, we weren't.

Just as Simon took the bucket, soap, sponges, and towels back toward the garage, a car pulled into the driveway.

It was another Toyota Camry, but this one was older and it was dark red.

The car stopped and the driver turned it off.

It was an old woman. It took her a little while to get out of the car. She had to swing both her legs out the door and set her feet on the driveway before standing up.

"Hey, Simon," Rosie called. He was almost to the garage. "Your grandma's here."

Simon turned around quickly with a huge smile on his face. You could tell he was really excited to see his grandma.

And then the smile disappeared completely. Simon took a few steps back toward us.

"That's not my grandma," he said in a quiet voice. It wasn't a whisper, but it was soft enough that only Rosie and I could hear him. "I've never seen that woman before in my life."

WHOOSH! YOU'VE ALREADY READ FIVE CHAPTERS. HOW MANY MORE CHAPTERS WILL YOU READ BEFORE YOU REST?

CHAPTER SIX

MYRTLE—RHYMES WITH TURTLE

SIMON PUT THE bucket down and the three of us walked toward her. We didn't know what to say. We didn't know who she was—or why she was there. It didn't matter. She spoke first.

"How much?" she asked real loud.

"Excuse me?" Rosie asked.

"I said, 'How much?'"

"Umm, I'm not sure what you mean," Rosie said slowly.

"Can we help you with something?"

"You have to speak up, missy!" the old woman called and brought her hand up to her ear. "I can't hear a doggone thing anymore. They gave me this dumb gadget to help me hear better! I'll tell you what I hear now. Buzzing! That's right: buzzing! Like there are mosquitoes having a party in my ear!"

"Umm," Rosie said.

"I don't have all day, kiddies," the woman said. "Can't you tell I'm as old as the hills? I remember when this whole area was a soybean farm. Soybeans! You know who eats soybeans? Cows and pigs and chickens! And then we eat the cows and pigs and chickens. Seems to me we ought to just eat the soybeans. Don't you think?"

"Yes," I said.

"What?" she yelled. "What did you say? I can't hear too good! Did I tell you that? Buzzing! Gosh-darned mosquitoes—that's what it sounds like!"

"Yes!" I repeated a lot louder. "Eating the soybeans first would make more sense. That would make the cows and pigs and chickens a lot happier too."

"Now you're talking! I like you three already!" the woman called. She waved her hand at the clean blue Toyota Camry

and then at her own red one. "My name is Myrtle. Rhymes with turtle. So, how much?"

Rosie figured it out first. She usually does.

"I think she wants us to wash her car," Rosie whispered.

It made sense to me and Simon then too.

"You want us to wash your car, ma'am? Umm, Myrtle?" Simon asked. He was talking loudly now too. We all were. It was kind of funny.

"Well, what do you think?" she yelled. "Why else would I be here? To buy groceries? Get gas? Harvest soybeans? Of course I want a car wash! That's why you're here, isn't it?"

"Umm, sure," Rosie answered loudly. Then in a lower voice she said to me and Simon, "I think we better just wash her car."

Simon and I both nodded.

"Okay, but we need to hurry up. Dad's getting closer every minute," Simon whispered to us. Then, in a louder voice,

he said to Myrtle, "You don't need to pay us."

"Don't be ridiculous! What kind of a business are you running here anyway?" the old lady asked. "They charge ten dollars down at Sudsy Sam's. It's not worth ten dollars, but it's the only car wash in town. They don't wash the hubcaps. I like hubcaps. I like mine shiny! Will you wash my hubcaps?"

43

"I think she might be a little crazy," Simon whispered.

"She's not crazy," Rosie giggled. "She's just old and funny."

"We'll wash your hubcaps!" I yelled.

SEVEN TOTAL CARS

WE WASHED MYRTLE'S car as she stood at the side of the driveway. She liked the way Simon and I gave Rosie a boost so she could reach the roof of the car. We were starting on the hubcaps when Myrtle called me over.

"Can you help me with this?" she asked and held her cell phone out to me. "I want to call my friend Joe. He lives at the Breezy Acres retirement home too."

"And you want to call him?"

"Yes, I do! Got something important to tell him," Myrtle said. "But I don't know how to use this doggone phone. My daughter got it for me. She put Joe's number in there somewhere. It's supposed to make life easier. Hogwash! That's what I say! It's like this hearing aid thingamajig. Sounds like buzzing! Like mosquitoes! Did I tell you that?"

"You did, yes."

"My name's Myrtle—rhymes with turtle," she told me again. Then she got a funny look on her face. She stared at the top of my head for a few seconds. "You remind me of my cat. Her name is Frenchie. Your hair reminds me of her fur. It has a wonderful sheen to it."

"Umm, thanks," I replied, because I didn't know what else to say. Nobody had ever, you know, compared me to a cat before.

I showed Myrtle how to use the home button to activate her phone. I found Joe's name on her Favorites screen and told her to touch it.

"Why should I touch his name?" Myrtle asked.

"That's how you call him."

"But where are the numbers?" she asked. She wasn't quite getting it yet. "You need numbers to call somebody! Everybody knows that!"

"The phone knows the number," I said. "Your daughter put it in there."

Myrtle touched Joe's name and I motioned for her to put the phone up to her ear.

"It's ringing!" she exclaimed. "By golly, it's ringing!"

Then I went to help Simon and Rosie with the hubcaps. I knew Myrtle wanted those hubcaps shiny. We could hear her talk to her friend Joe as we worked.

"Joe, it's Myrtle!" she said loudly. "Listen, I'm getting a car wash on Maple Avenue. Where the old soybean farm was. They cleaned the roof even though they can't reach it. You should have seen it! Bring your car over! It's filthy. Tell everybody at Breezy Acres!"

Rosie, Simon, and I all heard her.

"No," Simon whispered. "No, no, no. The garage will

never be clean by the time Dad gets home!"

When we finished, Myrtle paid us fifteen dollars—five dollars each. She told us we were better than Sudsy Sam's. We said goodbye and watched Myrtle pull slowly—very slowly—out of the driveway.

Simon said, "I wish my dad drove that slow."

As soon as Myrtle pulled out, Joe drove in.

And there were three cars behind his.

We washed Joe's car.

Then we washed cars for Harriet, Hazel, Becky, Archie, and Gladys.

We washed seven cars—and made fifteen dollars per car. Rosie did the math in her head. We made one hundred and five dollars. That worked out to thirty-five dollars for each of us.

$15 $15 $15 $15 $15 $15 $15

$105 TOTAL $105 ÷ 3 = $35

"That's more than I get for my birthday!" Simon said. He was pretty excited.

Rosie and I were too. It was a lot of money.

That's when Simon's mom came out again.

"My car looks great!" she said.

We told her we washed seven other cars. We told her we made one hundred and five dollars—and she whistled at such a big amount. Then we told her all about Myrtle. She thought it was super funny that Myrtle talked really loud and said her name rhymed with turtle, like, a million times.

"Mom?" Simon asked. "Can you show us where Dad is now?"

She did.

He was almost to Indianapolis.

We were running out of time.

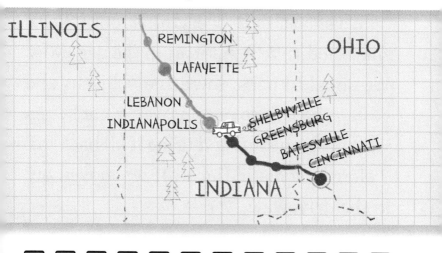

CHAPTER EIGHT

FLAMINGOS, COMIC BOOKS, AND BUNGEE CORDS

THE GARAGE WAS totally full of stuff.

"Where should we start?" Simon asked.

"Let's just pull everything out," Rosie suggested. "We'll put it all in the driveway. We should knock down the cobwebs and sweep the garage out anyway, right? Then we can clean stuff and bring it all back in."

Here is some of the stuff we moved out to the driveway:

Hammers, wrenches, and screwdrivers

Five old paint cans

Lots of gardening gloves

Empty flowerpots

A bucket of nails and screws

Three basketballs, two baseballs, a soccer ball, and seven tennis balls

Two stepladders

A stack of old newspapers

One big adult bike

Three brooms

Dozens of Simon's old comic books in a plastic box

Some cans of motor oil

Two rubber bins of Simon's old homework assignments and report cards

Three rakes

Eight plastic pink flamingos

Two shovels

An old Easter basket

Two bags of old clothes

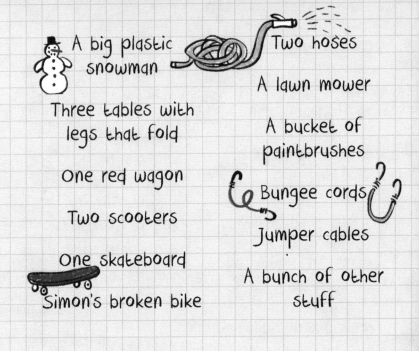

A big plastic snowman

Two hoses

A lawn mower

Three tables with legs that fold

A bucket of paintbrushes

One red wagon

Bungee cords

Two scooters

Jumper cables

One skateboard

Simon's broken bike

A bunch of other stuff

It took almost an hour to get everything out of the garage. Simon went to check with his mom. His dad was way closer. He was past Lafayette.

Simon and Rosie let me do the organizing. I like to organize things. My brain is good at it.

I put everything together in categories.

Some of them made perfect sense to Rosie and Simon. A bunch of outside stuff—two of the rakes, the hoses, and gardening things—were grouped together. And I grouped Simon's stuff—the balls, skateboard, and his broken bike—all together.

But some of the groups didn't make as much sense to them.

Here's an example: the motor oil, the Easter basket, a broom, a rake, and the adult bike.

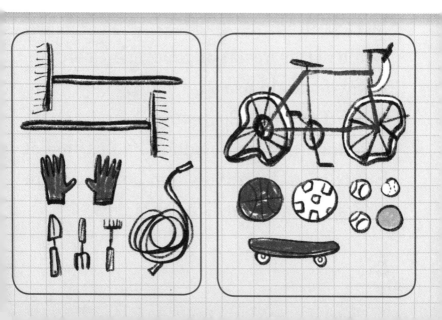

Rosie asked, "Why are these things grouped together?"

I thought it was kind of funny that they couldn't tell why. I mean, it was obvious to me.

"It's *The Wizard of Oz* group," I answered.

"*The Wizard of Oz?*" Simon asked. "How?"

"Well, the Tin Man needed to be oiled all the time, so that's the motor oil," I explained and pointed at each item. "Dorothy rode around on her bike and carried Toto in a basket. The Wicked Witch of the West rode around on a broom. And you could use a rake for sweeping up straw. That's the Scarecrow."

Simon and Rosie nodded and smiled at me. They really understand how my brain works. It made sense to them now.

We put a lot of stuff on the three tables after we unfolded the legs. The rest we just put on the driveway.

Once everything was organized, we each took a broom and knocked a bunch of cobwebs and dust off the garage walls, corners, and ceiling. It took a while. We didn't see any actual spiders.

When that was done, we swept the floor.

We built up a big cloud of dust and *whooooshed* it out the door—and away from the newly washed car. The dust cloud was so thick that we could barely see through it.

When that big dust cloud settled, we could see better.

We couldn't believe what we saw.

WHOA! WHAT DO YOU THINK THEY'LL SEE?

CHAPTER NINE

HOW MUCH?

THERE WERE THREE people in Simon's driveway.

There was a woman about my mom's age. She had a boy with her. He was younger than a kindergartner but big enough to walk without falling down. There was also an older kid, like a teenager. He looked like he was in high school or college.

He was the one who saw us come out of the garage. He called to us, "How much?"

"What?" Simon called back.

The teenager pointed down at something on the driveway and asked again, "How much?"

We couldn't see what he was pointing at because the blue Toyota Camry was in the way.

"How much what?" Simon asked as we got closer.

The teenager leaned down and picked up one of the bright-pink flamingos.

"How much for a flamingo?" he asked a third time. "This would look awesome in my dorm room."

"Umm, I don't know," Simon said.

Rosie was the first to figure it out. Again.

"They think it's a garage sale," she said. "They think the stuff in the driveway is all for sale."

"No way," Simon said.

"Way," Rosie answered and laughed a little.

"I'll be right back," Simon said and ran into the house.

"He'll, umm, be back," I called to the teenager.

"Okay," he said, shrugged, and put the flamingo down. He started to look through some of Simon's comic books.

Simon came out of his house with his mom. He waved to us, and Rosie and I ran over.

Simon explained to his mom that the people in the driveway thought we were having a garage sale.

"I've been trying to get rid of that stuff for years. But your father wouldn't let me," she said and laughed. She was making fun of Simon's dad without being mean. "If there's more than one of something, you can sell it. And you can keep whatever you make."

"Really?" Simon asked.

"Really."

"What about the prices?" Simon asked.

"You three are smart. You'll figure it out," his mom answered and then pulled her phone out of her pocket. She looked at it for a few seconds. "You better get moving though. Dad's almost to Remington."

We ran back to the driveway.

And we had a garage sale.

CHAPTER TEN

COUNTING
THE CASH

SIMON GOT THE teenager's attention. He pointed to the pile of eight pink plastic flamingos and said, "Three dollars each."

The teenager thought that was fine and said, "I'll take two. And how about the comic books?"

"How about twenty-five cents each?"

"Sure."

The mom stood by the flamingos and

said, "I'll take one of these too."

She picked out a pink flamingo and handed it to her son. He started chewing on its yellow plastic beak for some reason.

Some high school girls bought a bunch of Simon's dad's old shirts. They said they looked retro.

We also sold a hose, one scooter, one table with folding legs, four more pink flamingos, one rake, almost all the comic books, one broom, some flowerpots, and one stepladder.

It took over an hour. And by that time, Simon's dad was in Crown Point, Indiana.

When we were sure nobody else was coming, we wiped everything down with wet towels and put it all back in the garage. It was a lot cleaner and there was a lot less stuff.

Simon pushed the final thing—his broken bike—into the garage's farthest back corner. It was kind of sad and funny how the bike wobbled and clunked on its flat tires and dented wheel rims.

After Simon leaned the bike against the wall, he joined Rosie and me.

Simon pulled two big wads of money and a bunch of change out of his pockets. He dumped it all on the garage floor.

"How much do you think we made from the garage sale?" he asked, looking down and watching one of the quarters roll to a stop. "It looks like a lot."

"It does," I said.

"It's eighty-one dollars and seventy-five cents," Rosie said. "I kept track."

Simon and I knew we didn't need to count the money. If Rosie said it was eighty-one dollars and seventy-five cents, then it was eighty-one dollars and seventy-five cents.

"How much is that for each of us?" asked Simon.

And, of course, Rosie knew. She said, "It's twenty-seven dollars and twenty-five cents apiece. And we each made thirty-five dollars at the car wash. So that means we have sixty-two dollars and twenty-five cents each. That's a total of one hundred and eighty-six dollars and seventy-five cents."

$27.25 + $35 = $62.25
$62.25 + $62.25 + $62.25 = $186.75

We all smiled at each other. It was a ton of money.

"Will you two sort it all out and divide it and stuff?" Simon said and pointed down at the pile of money. "I'm going to get Mom so she can see the finished job."

After Simon left, Rosie crouched down and started to separate the bills into stacks of singles, fives, and tens.

But I stopped her.

I grabbed her right hand.

She looked up at me.

I pointed toward the back of the garage and said, "I have an idea."

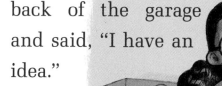

CHAPTER ELEVEN

FIFTY PIZZAS AND TWENTY MILKSHAKES

SIMON'S MOM LOOKED at the garage and said we did an excellent job. She congratulated us on making the money.

We realized right then that we were all starving. All that work made us super hungry.

"We should go for pizza or ice cream," Rosie suggested.

"Can I?" Simon asked his mom. "Where's Dad?"

"He's in Hammond," his mom said after checking her phone. "That's about an hour and a half away. You can make it back in time."

We were all happy about that.

"Should we get pizza or ice cream?" Simon asked as we walked to town. "We're like millionaires! We could get both!"

"Maybe," Rosie said and caught my eye when Simon wasn't looking. She winked at me.

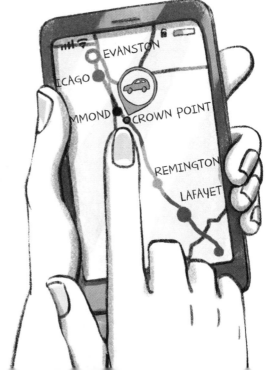

"Yeah," I said and winked back. "Maybe."

"We have enough money to get, like, fifty pizzas and twenty milkshakes!" Simon said. He was excited. I think he thought maybe—just maybe—he wouldn't get into too much trouble with his dad now. "Where should we go first?"

We didn't stop at the pizza place first.

And we didn't stop at the ice cream shop first.

We stopped at Sycamore Sports first.

It was a store that had loads of sports stuff and camping stuff.

And bikes.

"Why are we going in here?" Simon asked.

Rosie said, "I want to look for some-thing."

She walked straight to the bikes at the back of the store. There was a high school kid working there. He had a bike up on a rack and was spinning its front tire.

"Can I help you three?" he asked.

Rosie did the talking.

"We're looking for a mountain bike," Rosie said.

Simon hadn't figured it out yet. He just watched Rosie with a puzzled look on his face.

"We've got a few models," the teenager said and walked us over to a wall where a bunch of bikes were lined up. He waved at them as he described them.

"These are the Rock Jumpers—good basic mountain bike. These are Trail Hunters—about the same, just a little sturdier. And the top of the line is the Mongoose. It has an aluminum frame instead of steel. Much lighter, but twice as strong. Can really take the bumps."

Rosie asked, "How much is the Mongoose?"

"It's expensive."

"How much?"

"It's 145 dollars."

"Do you have an orange one?"

"I do."

"We'll take it."

He went to get the bike.

Simon still hadn't figured it out.

He asked, "What's going on?"

"We're getting you a new bike!" Rosie said. "One that won't get all busted up on

the trails at Picasso Park. It was Molly's idea!"

I could see tears welling up in Simon's eyes. He was so surprised. And so happy.

ONLY ONE MORE
CHAPTER TO GO!
ARE YOU FEELING AS
GOOD AS SIMON?

CHAPTER TWELVE

SIMON'S DAD COMES HOME

WE HAD ENOUGH money left over for pizza.

Simon insisted on sitting in the front window at Pequod's Pizza. He wanted to keep an eye on his new bike.

We got an extra-large pepperoni pizza and three large lemonades. Since I only eat things in even numbers, I like pepperoni pizza the best. That's because it's easy to count the pepperoni slices. If it's not an even number I can just take one off, easy peasy.

We ate the whole thing.

And we drank all the lemonade.

And then Rosie and I ran along on each side of Simon as he rode his new bike home. He probably wanted to go real fast—who wouldn't want to go fast on a brand-new bike?!—but he didn't. He went slow so we didn't have to run too hard.

When we were about one block from his house, Simon's dad passed us in his car. He honked and waved.

Simon stopped his bike on the sidewalk. It was so new that the brakes made a rubbery squeaky sound.

"Wish me luck," Simon said. I could tell he was getting nervous again.

"Good luck," Rosie and I said at the same time.

We didn't go with him, but we sort of stood behind a clump of trees and watched from a distance.

We couldn't hear what happened. We were too far away.

But we could see what happened.

Simon parked his new bike in the driveway after his dad pulled into the garage. His mom came out and stood on the porch. When his dad came out of the garage, he was smiling and shaking his head.

Simon used his hands as he talked. He pointed at his mom's clean car and up the street toward the Breezy Acres retirement home.

He held up seven fingers to show how many cars we washed. I think he told his dad all about the garage sale then, because he waved his hands toward the driveway. Finally, Simon pointed at his brand-new bike.

Then he shoved his hands in his pockets and hung his head a little bit.

"Do you think he's telling him about getting into trouble at school now?" Rosie asked.

"I think so."

His dad nodded his head and rubbed Simon's hair. Then he put his arm around Simon's shoulders and kind of steered him into the garage.

"What's happening now?" I asked Rosie.
"I don't know."

A minute later, Simon's dad came out of the garage riding the adult bike. He called something over to Simon's mom. Simon hurried to his new bike and hopped on.

They rode side by side out of the driveway and turned right.

That's the way to Picasso Park.

HIGH FIVE!

You've read **12** chapters,

87 pages,

and **6,194** words!

Way to go! Do you feel amazing?

6,194 words? If you took 6,194 steps, you'd walk more than two miles.

I think I'll go eat some Cocoa Puffs.

Fun and Games!

THINK

Molly, Rosie, and Simon think Myrtle (rhymes with turtle) is charming and funny. Do you know any silly-acting grown-ups? What's the wackiest thing they do? What's that person's first name? Can you rhyme that name with other words?

FEEL

Simon totally loves Cocoa Puffs. What's your favorite food? Would you walk five miles to get it? How would you feel when you got your favorite food and ate it? Can you draw your favorite food—and the expression on your face when you got to eat it?

ACT

There is a ton of stuff in Simon's garage. Do you have extra things in your room? Maybe you have clothes that don't fit or toys you don't play with anymore. Do you know someone who could use and enjoy those things? Is there a place in your town where you could donate them?

Tom Watson is the author of the popular STICK DOG and STICK CAT series. And now he's the author of this new series, TROUBLE AT TABLE 5. Tom lives in Chicago with his wife and kids and their big dog, Shadow. When he's not at home, Tom's usually out visiting classrooms all over the country. He's met a lot of students who remind him of Molly, Simon, and Rosie. He's learned that kids are smarter than adults. Like, way smarter.

Marta Kissi is originally from Warsaw but now lives in London where she loves bringing stories to life. She shares her art studio with her husband, James, and their pet plant, Trevor.